CW00738817

THE MYSTERY OF THE MISSING LUNCH

CRIME FIGHTERS CLUB #1

JORDAN WINTERS

Text Copyright © 2022 Jordan Winters

Illustrations Copyright © 2022 Courtney O-Brien

All rights reserved.

ISBN 979-8-9863662-0-3 (paperback)

ISBN 979-8-9863662-1-0 (hardback)

Also available as an ebook!

Library of Congress Control Number: 2022914752

Published by Beyond Adventure Books

beyondadventurebooks.com

Instagram: @beyondadventurebooks

Twitter: @BeyondAdvBooks

Facebook: @beyondadventurebooks

Cover design by GetCovers

Illustrations by Courtney O-Brien

Typeset by Chelsea Jackson, Jackson Writing and Editing, LLC

Dedicated to all kids who have wanted to solve a mystery.

Table of Contents

1

The Bully

"Put that down!"

"Make me!"

"Don't think I can't!"

The Edison Elementary School playground immediately reacted to the sounds that could only mean one thing: a fight! Kids swarmed from everywhere. They swung down off the jungle gym, tunneled through the tube slide, and pushed through the crowd. Before long, the two culprits had a big audience.

7

"I said put that down, Mikey, lard-for-brains!"

A chase immediately followed, and the students ended up in the school hallway.

Marybeth had her hands on her hips. Her friends always knew that she was serious when she had her hands on her hips. Her opponent held a spiral-bound notebook over his head. He was at least a foot taller than Marybeth and much heavier, even though they were in the same class.

"I've got it, and you don't! I've got it, and you don't!" Mikey taunted.

Although he might have had the advantage on her in height, Marybeth had accurately chosen her insult. As she yelled at him, and her classmates hooted and hollered, her friend Akari sneaked up behind him.

Mikey wasn't the only one taller than Marybeth. Akari was too. With just a little hop, she snatched the notebook out of his hands.

"Hey!" Mikey said.

Mikey turned around, surprised to lose his treasure and his taunt at the same time. Akari stuck her tongue out at him and ran off behind the crowd. The kids now laughed at Mikey instead of Marybeth.

"I guess now I've got it, and you don't," Marybeth said.

The bell rang to end morning recess. The kids scattered, seeing the teachers heading toward them.

The kids filed into Mrs. Stardowski's class quietly. Marybeth's eyes still shot daggers at Mikey as she hugged her notebook protectively. She was glad to have her most important possession back.

"Don't worry, Marybeth. We'll get him back!" Akari said.

Marybeth nodded. She could always trust Akari to have her back. Marybeth, Ariel, and Akari had been best friends since first grade. The three girls were nothing alike. Marybeth liked details, Ariel liked to watch people, and Akari always looked for clues. They didn't always get along, but they always made up when they had a fight. The best thing about best friends is that they stick together.

Mrs. Stardowski had arranged the desks into groups that she called pods. In Marybeth's pod, none of her friends sat near her. She suspected that Mrs. Stardowski did that on purpose. Instead, Marybeth had a quiet boy named Noah as a seatmate.

The rest of the pod was made up of Natasha, who sat across from Marybeth, and Deshawn, who was probably the second quietest boy in the class other than Noah. Mrs. Stardowski must have figured that if anyone could get them to talk, it would be Marybeth.

After recess, the class was supposed to sit at their desks and write quietly. Marybeth opened her notebook and scribbled furiously about the incident on the playground. She also drew a picture of Mickey next to the description.

When she finished, she caught Akari's eye across the room. Akari knew exactly what she was doing. It was always best to collect evidence when it was fresh in a person's mind, even if the culprit had already been brought to justice. Next to Mikey's picture, Marybeth wrote *case solved*. She knew who had spied on her and her friends during recess. Of course, it was Mikey, the bully.

2
Missing Lunch

That day's math lesson was boooring. Marybeth didn't like fractions, except when her teacher talked about pie, and that just made her hungry. As soon as Mrs. Stardowski dismissed her pod, Marybeth rushed to the little alcove at the back of the room where the class kept their lunches.

"Hey! I can't find my lunch bag!"

The cry was muffled because the kid who

said it was crouched down on the floor behind several of Marybeth's classmates. Marybeth was immediately curious. She grabbed her notebook from her bookbag.

"Who said that? Whose lunch is missing?" Marybeth asked loudly above the crowd while opening her notebook.

"Mine!"

D'Maryea popped out from behind the crowd of kids jockeying for their lunches. He was not amused by Marybeth's professional attitude. He put his hands on top of his head and pretended to pull at his hair, which was impossible because he kept it in short waves on his head.

"When and where did you last see your lunch today?" Marybeth asked.

"Where do you think?" he said, pointing to the shelf next to the coat racks.

"Okay, fair enough. Are you sure that is where you last saw it?" Marybeth asked.

"Marybeth!" D'Maryea stomped. The kids around him scattered at the irritation in his voice. "I always put my lunch RIGHT THERE, next to my coat."

"You don't need to shout," Marybeth told him. "Could you describe for me what your lunch bag looks like?" Marybeth asked, continuing to write down everything.

"My lunch bag is the same one as Mikey's, except his has green trim and mine has red," described D'Maryea quickly.

"Interesting. You have never gotten your lunch bags mixed up before," she said, wondering if solving the mystery would be easy after all.

"There was one day . . . but when I opened my bag, I realized immediately it was his. He ate half of my lunch before he noticed," said D'Maryea with obvious irritation.

Marybeth wrote all of this down carefully while also trying to draw a diagram of the scene in her notebook.

"Can you walk outside and walk back in to show me just how you put it down?" Marybeth asked.

D'Maryea's face darkened. He seemed ready to explode, and Marybeth wisely moved on.

"Okay, never mind that. Can you remember the last time you saw your lunch? Did you see it when you walked out to recess or came back into the classroom after recess?" Marybeth asked.

This calmed D'Maryea down a bit.

"I don't remember seeing it. Not before or after. It could have been there, but I don't know. I don't usually check to make sure my lunch is where I put it each morning!" D'Maryea said, getting worked up again.

Marybeth snapped her notebook shut and slapped her pen against it. "Ah-ha!"

"What's 'ah-ha'?" D'Maryea asked.

Marybeth did not want to admit to D'Maryea that she was not sure. She also realized she had an audience. Two or three other students milled around, pretending like they were not listening, and, of course, Akari and Ariel were there to support her.

"Obviously, someone swiped your lunch at recess," Marybeth said.

Her classmates whispered around her, and Mikey's name was the loudest.

"Stealing a person's lunch during recess?"

"His bullying has reached a new level."

"Wow."

"This has happened before."

"What?" Marybeyth turned around.

Santiago nodded. "It's not the first time. Every few days, it's someone different."

DeMaryea and the other boys nodded.

"That's it!" Maybeth said. "We have to solve the mystery of the missing lunch. This can't go on!"

"Marybeth? D'Maryea? What is going on here?"

Mrs. Stardowski had noticed the gathering of students at the lunchboxes and came to see what was going on. She walked purposefully toward them.

"Mrs. Stardowski, someone stole D'Maryea's lunch. It's been happening a lot. But don't worry. We're on the case!"

THE MYSTERY OF THE MISSING LUNCH

3
The Crime Fighters Club

"Who is on the case?" Mrs. Stardowski asked. She seemed very confused. Marybeth could understand that. After all, she was the teacher. But when it came to knowing what happened inside the classroom, teachers couldn't be expected to know everything.

"The Crime Fighters Club, Mrs. Stardowski!" Marybeth said, even though no such club existed. She looked from her notebook to

D'Maryea, the victim, to Mrs. Stardowski. Something had to be done fast, and her teacher would not be the one to do it.

"I see," Mrs. Stardowski said.

That was the tone all teachers used to let their students know they were still kids. It didn't stop Marybeth, though. She was going to find out who stole D'Maryea's lunch, and she was going to do it fast.

First, she needed clues, which she had already begun to collect. Then she would interview witnesses. Next, she would . . . what was next?

"It's okay, Mrs. Stardowski. My mom always packs too much. I can share," Akari said.

Akari's offer had interrupted Marybeth's thoughts. Looking up at her, Marybeth saw that Akari just wanted to get out of there. Plus, Akari always had healthy food when she'd rather have chips and sweets. Looking around at the other kids, Marybeth figured they all probably saw the minutes of lunch ticking by.

"That is very kind of you, Akari. Is that all right with you, D'Maryea?" Mrs. Stardowski asked.

"Sure. But I still want to know who took my lunch!" D'Maryea said with irritation.

D'Maryea sent Marybeth a look that she determined meant only one thing: *find out who took my lunch!*

As the other students filed out of class, Marybeth practically bounced up and down. She even forgot to get her own lunch. Fortunately, Akari was used to Marybeth getting distracted and grabbed both lunches before they went outside.

After Akari gave D'Maryea some of her lunch, Marybeth, Akari, and Ariel found a spot on the grass to sit down and eat. It was a sunny spring day, and everyone was eating outside. Marybeth made sure that they sat where they could see the classroom door. She ate with her sandwich in one hand and her notebook in the other.

"What is the Crime Fighters Club?" Akari asked as she popped a chunk of pepper in her mouth. Her parents worked in a restaurant, which was why she always had healthy food for lunch.

"We are!" Marybeth said.

"We?" Akari asked.

Marybeth was surprised that her friends were not more on board with her idea. But then, sometimes she had to explain things and give them time to catch up. After all, her ideas often got a little ahead of her explanations.

"You, me, and Ariel," Marybeth answered, pointing to each of them.

With a bag of chips in her hand, Ariel looked at Marybeth through long eyelashes. She was a careful thinker. While she was usually willing to go along with Marybeth's plans, it often took more convincing and more time to get Ariel to agree. After chewing and swallowing, she pushed her long, flowing brown hair behind her eye and sat up straight. This gesture often meant that Ariel had made up her mind.

"Why did you get to decide on a club? Why are you always the boss?" Ariel asked.

"Oh, come on, Ariel! I just thought of it is all!" Marybeth answered.

Marybeth was a little hurt by Ariel's reaction. She had hoped her friends would be as excited by the club as she was. The truth was she needed them. She wasn't sure how she would catch the thief without them. She needed to find something to convince Ariel and Akari to join.

"Don't you want to be a founding member?" Marybeth asked Ariel.

"Founding member? What's that?" This seemed to catch Ariel's attention. Even Akari seemed interested. The problem was, Marybeth had no idea what it meant to be a founding member of the Crime Fighters Club. She had made it up, probably from something she read somewhere.

"It means *we* get to make the rules!" Akari told her friends.

Akari seemed quite sure of herself. Secretly, Marybeth was glad Akari had said it. At least one of them knew what she was doing! Now all they had to do was get together and solve their first crime—who was stealing the lunches.

4
Club Rules

The girls decided that before they could start investigating, the Crime Fighters Club needed rules. After much discussion, they set the first five rules. Marybeth was firm on the need to start with five rules, so five was what they had.

Rule #1: All clues must be written down.

Rule #2: All suspects are innocent until proven guilty.

Rule #3: No adults allowed!

Rule #4: If things get scary, we will tell an adult.

Rule #5: All club members will vote on new members.

Marybeth had chosen rule #3, but Ariel insisted on rule #4. What she said was that Marybeth's rule #3 was dangerous, so they added rule #4.

Now that they had club rules, it was time to investigate. The girls had finished their lunch, so they carried their lunch bags into the classroom. Their teacher was at the back of the room. Marybeth had her notebook and pen ready. The girls gathered around the spot where D'Maryea had said he last saw his lunch bag.

"You know what we need? We need some of that special tape that they put around crime scenes!" Marybeth said.

"Marybeth! We don't have any of that!" Akari said.

"Akari, how will we keep people out of the crime scene if we don't block it off?" Marybeth asked.

"I know!" Akari said. She left and came back with a long jump rope. She tied it around the lunch bag area.

"Oh boy, Akari! That's great," Marybeth said.

"I don't know if Mrs. Stardowski will like this," Ariel said.

"It's okay, Ariel. Mrs. Stardowski wants us to catch the thief," Marybeth said.

Marybeth put her hands on her hips and surveyed the scene carefully. She wished she had a magnifying glass like Nancy Drew. How was she supposed to find clues without a magnifying glass? Marybeth slapped herself on the forehead and went over to the science supplies and came back with three magnifying glasses.

"What are these for?" Ariel asked.

"They are for finding clues! Haven't you read *Nancy Drew*, Ariel?" Marybeth asked.

Ariel nodded, and the girls started looking for clues.

Suddenly, Akari shrieked and exclaimed, "I found something! Look at this, everyone!"

The girls scrambled over to Akari then scrunched down on the floor under the shelf. Sure enough, there was something there.

D'Maryea's lunch bag!

5
New Club Members

"What are you guys doing in here?" Deshawn asked.

Marybeth, Ariel, and Akari spun around. Deshawn and Santiago stood in the doorway. The two boys looked suspiciously at the girls.

"We are finding out who stole D'Maryea's lunch. What else?" Akari stood up quickly and went up to the boys. "What are *you* doing here?"

"We had the same idea," Deshawn said.

"You did?" Akari asked doubtfully.

"Yes. D'Maryea is our friend," Deshawn said.

Akari and Deshawn stood almost toe to toe, glaring at each other. Neither one blinked or moved. They seemed to try to decide whether to believe the other. Finally, Marybeth broke the tension.

"Let's not get carried away. We all want to get to the bottom of this," Marybeth said.

Ariel raised an eyebrow at Marybeth. She liked to do that because she knew Marybeth couldn't.

"In fact—we can do it together! Do you want to join our new club?" Marybeth asked.

"I thought you said we all had to vote in new club members," Ariel said.

"Club? What club?" Santiago asked.

Deshawn took a step back so that he and Akari stood farther apart. He looked relieved.

Marybeth knew Deshawn hated conflict.

"Ariel's right. It's a new club. Ariel, Akari, and I just founded it to investigate crimes at Edison Elementary School—and beyond!" Marybeth said.

Marybeth looked at Ariel and Akari. She didn't know what to do. The rules said all members had to vote in new members. The rules did not say she couldn't describe the club to potential new members, though.

She added that last bit as a second thought because it sounded good in her head. After all, if they solved their first case quickly enough, maybe they could take on cases from the neighborhood. The sky would be the limit!

Ariel snickered. She was used to Marybeth getting carried away. Marybeth shrugged. It was good to have friends who knew her so well.

"That sounds fun. How do we join?" Santiago asked.

"Wait a minute, Santiago. We have rules!" Marybeth said.

She pulled out her notebook, and in her most proper teacher voice, she read the rules.

Club Rules

Rule 1: All clues must be written down.

Rule 2: All suspects are innocent until proven guilty.

Rule 3: No adults allowed!

Rule 4: If things get scary, we will tell an adult.

Rule 5: All club members will vote on new members.

New Club Members

The boys listened politely, and Akari and Ariel nodded their heads. Then Deshawn wrinkled his brow in confusion.

"Why do you need rule #3 if you have rule #4?" Deshawn asked.

Marybeth rolled her eyes. "We may need to revise some of these rules. So, give us a minute. We need to vote," Marybeth told him.

The boys nodded, and the girls huddled. They felt a little in over their heads. Some new club members might be just what they needed.

"Okay, boys, you're in!" Marybeth said.

Santiago and Deshawn met Marybeth's announcement with proud and serious expressions, and everyone shook hands.

6
The First Clue

Marybeth wasted no time getting the boys up to speed on the case.

"This is our first clue. We found D'Maryea's lunch bag. The thief left it here, under the shelves on the floor," Marybeth told them.

Ariel lifted the jump-rope barricade so Santiago and Deshawn could come into the crime scene. There, the five Crime Fighters reviewed their evidence. Marybeth gave

Santiago her magnifying glass so she could take notes. Deshawn used two pencils to hold up the lunch bag so he would not directly touch it.

"Wow, Deshawn. That's really smart!" Marybeth said.

"Oh, I saw it on TV," Deshawn said.

"Now we need D'Maryea to tell us if anything is missing," Santiago said.

Once they had the lunch bag where they could inspect it, they reviewed the contents. Marybeth made a list of the evidence in her notebook.

"What do you think it means?" Ariel asked.

The contents stumped everyone. It was a strange collection of items to have left behind. Marybeth tried to think of what Nancy Drew would do.

"What can we learn from what's left in the lunch bag?" Marybeth asked.

> ⸏ **Evidence List** ⸏
> ───────
>
> **Evidence:** D'Maryea's Lunch Bag
>
> **Location Found:** under
>
> the shelves in the alcove
>
> **Contents:**
>
> 1-crumbled paper 🌑
>
> 1-candy wrapper 🍬
>
> 1-peanut butter sandwich 🍞

"He's not hungry!" Ariel said.

"How do you know?" Deshawn asked.

"How do you know the thief is a *he*?" Santiago asked.

Everyone talked at once. Marybeth's head hurt. No one was in charge of the club, but someone had to be in charge of the crime scene, and she held the notebook.

"Okay, Ariel. What makes you think *the thief* was not hungry?" Marybeth asked.

"He left the sandwich! That's what I would eat first if I was hungry," Ariel said.

"Hmm. That makes sense," Marybeth said.

All the club members nodded their heads.

"Wait a minute!" Santiago clapped his hands as if he had a big idea. "What if the thief just doesn't like peanut butter?"

"Some people are allergic to peanut butter," Akari said.

They both had good points, so Marybeth wrote them down. Akari said that maybe the thief was allergic to peanut butter, and Ariel said that maybe the thief just wasn't hungry.

They all wondered which one it was.

"If the thief was allergic to peanut butter, he would not have touched anything in there. My little cousin is allergic, and he can't go anywhere near peanuts," Santiago said.

"Good point, Santiago. Okay, so we have learned two things about the thief. He does not like peanut butter, and he is not allergic to it," Marybeth said.

"Not really, Marybeth. Maybe he just didn't read the candy bar label!" Deshawn said.

"If he was allergic to peanut butter, he wouldn't even look in the bag," Marybeth said.

They all stood there, staring at the items in front of them. Their questions stumped them. Suddenly, Santiago knew what they needed to do.

"We need to interview the victim!" Santiago said, looking at D'Maryea who just walked into the classroom.

THE MYSTERY OF THE MISSING LUNCH

7

The Victim's Interview

When lunch ended, Mrs. Stardowski asked them to take down their jump-rope-crime-scene tape. She suggested that since they had already found the lunch bag, they did not need it anymore.

Marybeth was put out by this, but since the teacher was in charge, she had no choice. They returned the lunch bag to D'Maryea, who was thrilled to have it back. Mikey seemed relieved not to be accused of being the thief.

At the end of the day, the class had gym. After the class walked or ran laps around the playground, they had free time. The Crime Fighters gathered and waited for D'Maryea to finish and then called him over to a bench shaded by a tree. Since he wanted to find the thief too, he agreed to the interview.

"So, D'Maryea, when was the last time you saw your lunch bag before it went missing?" Marybeth asked.

"You *already* asked me that," D'Maryea said.

"I know. But now that the Crime Fighters Club is on the case, I want to make sure we go back to the beginning. You might remember more details about it since then too."

D'Maryea raised his eyebrows but nodded.

"The last time I saw it was before recess. I left it on the shelf next to the coats, like I always do," D'Maryea said.

Marybeth nodded, writing this down.

Santiago raised his hand and stepped forward. Marybeth nodded toward him to show that he should go next.

"Does your lunch bag look like anyone else's besides Mikey's? Could *anyone else* have gotten it mixed up or taken it, thinking it was theirs?" Santiago asked.

"No one else has a lunch bag like mine, except for Mikey," answered D'Maryea.

"Is it possible that you forgot your lunch at home this morning?" asked Akari. "Maybe the one we found is a different lunch bag. Do you have more than one?"

There was a murmur among the other Crime Fighters at this question. None of them had thought of this. Marybeth looked up from writing. It was a pretty good question!

"No," D'Maryea said. "Who has two of the same lunch bags?"

"Lots of people do," Marybeth said, to avoid an argument. "Or they could. Your bag is the same as Mikey's."

"That was my bag," D'Maryea said.

"Okay."

Making a note of that, Marybeth looked up to see if anyone had a question to ask next. No one did, so she asked one of her own.

"Can you list the contents of your lunch bag?" Marybeth asked.

"Huh?" D'Maryea said.

"Do you know what was in your lunch bag this morning when you brought it to school?" Marybeth repeated.

"Oh. No, I didn't look inside," D'Maryea said.

The Crime Fighters looked disappointed.

"Who packs it?" Akari asked.

"My mom," D'Maryea said.

"What does she usually put in there then? Does she usually pack about the same things?" Marybeth asked.

D'Maryea thought about this for a minute.

"I don't know. Not really. I guess she packs whatever is around. She packs me a sandwich, some chips, and usually fruit. I doubt my mom even remembers what she put in there," D'Maryea said.

Deshawn asked, "Does your lunch ever have two sandwiches?"

D'Maryea looked at him like he was crazy. "Why would I have two sandwiches?" he replied.

"We are trying to figure out why the thief took some items and left the rest," Marybeth said.

The six of them looked around at one another for a moment, trying to decide what to do next. Marybeth rocked back and forth on the heels of her feet and chewed on the end of her pen. How would they solve this case without knowing the contents of the lunch bag?

"Let's return to the scene of the crime!" Marybeth said.

They all followed Marybeth back to the classroom, where they entered the alcove and pulled out D'Maryea's lunch bag. She opened it carefully and removed all the contents. Suddenly, D'Maryea grabbed the crumpled paper and stuck it in his pocket.

"Hey! That's evidence!" Marybeth said.

"It is not! It's private," D'Maryea said.

Seeing the look on D'Maryea's face, Marybeth decided not to push him. He looked embarrassed. He was a quiet boy, and she didn't want to cause him any more pain than the day's events already had given him.

"I'm sorry, D'Maryea. We saw it in your

lunch bag, but we didn't read it. I promise," Marybeth told him.

"It has nothing to do with the . . . case," D'Maryea said.

Ariel stepped forward and patted her classmate awkwardly on the back, trying to comfort him. Santiago did a better job.

"Hey, man, it's okay. We all have secrets. You just tell us it wasn't from the thief, and we'll leave it alone," Santiago said.

They all noticed that D'Maryea was looking at the floor.

"What is it, D'Maryea?" Marybeth asked.

"My ma, she writes me notes. This morning it wasn't crumpled."

THE MYSTERY OF THE MISSING LUNCH

8
Frustrating Clues

When Marybeth arrived in class the next morning, she was cranky. She had been up all night thinking about two clues and what they meant. She knew they meant something but wasn't sure what.

Important and Confusing Clue #1: The Sandwich

Why had the thief taken almost everything out of the bag and left the sandwich? Was he not hungry? Did he not like peanut butter? Was there another reason?

Important and Confusing Clue #2: The Note

Why would anyone crumple up a note from a boy's momma? The note would not have any importance to anyone except for D'Maryea and his mother. Why crumple it and then leave it?

Neither of these clues made any sense to Marybeth, and they were driving her crazy. She had been up half the night scribbling in her notebook until her mother saw her light on and threatened to take her notebook away. Marybeth had finally decided that she wasn't getting anywhere and tried to go to sleep. Instead, she had stared at the ceiling for a long time, just thinking.

In the morning, Marybeth was tired but couldn't wait to get to school. She stood outside the classroom waiting for the rest of the Crime Fighters to arrive. The first one there was Santiago.

"Hey, I have an idea." She grabbed his arm excitedly.

Marybeth opened her notebook to the list of clues from yesterday and showed it to him. She pointed to the diagram she had carefully drawn of the crime scene. There was an X where they had found D'Maryea's lunch bag.

"I think I know why the lunch bag was on the floor," Marybeth said.

"Why?" Santiago asked.

Santiago looked at the diagram curiously. He took a banana out of his lunch bag and munched on it. When he made no further comment, Marybeth went on.

"Everyone assumed that the thief just tossed the lunch bag down when he was done with it, right? But maybe he dropped it, and he wasn't really done with it!" Marybeth told him.

With that last statement, Marybeth looked at Santiago with a face full of triumph. Santiago did not seem impressed.

"He?" Santiago said.

"Huh?" Marybeth said.

"How come you keep saying 'he'? It could have been a *she*? How do you know a boy stole D'Maryea's lunch?" Santiago said.

Chewing her lip in frustration, Marybeth glared at Santiago. He seemed to be completely missing the point. She shook her head.

"It doesn't matter! *He, she*, whatever!" Marybeth said.

"Just because D'Maryea is a boy does not mean that it was a boy that stole his lunch, you know," Santiago said.

Marybeth was beginning to think Santiago was like a dog with a bone. He just would not

Frustrating Clues

let it go. She wished there was another word in English that meant "neither he nor she."

"Something or someone startled *THE THIEF*, and THE THIEF dropped the lunch before . . . finishing with it," Marybeth said.

Santiago nodded. He smiled even though Marybeth had shouted at him. They needed to catch this thief before there were any more grammar lessons or arguments about the rights of boys and girls.

"How did the thief get interrupted? Does that mean we have another witness? Someone who did not come forward?" Marybeth said.

"I don't know. It seems like if someone had seen the thief in action, we would have known," Santiago said.

The two Crime Fighters stood in silence, reviewing the case. Ariel and Deshawn walked up, and Santiago and Marybeth quickly caught them up on their discussion and the new question they were worrying about. By the time Akari had joined them, they still had not solved the puzzle.

"Do you think someone walked in and startled the thief, and the person does not even know what happened? Maybe our witness does not even know he's a witness," Akari said.

"*He* or *she*!" Santiago said.

Marybeth groaned. "Santiago's right. Whether it was a girl or boy, we need to find out who walked in on the thief. That person might have important evidence."

Getting out her notebook, Marybeth decided it was best to divide and conquer. All the Crime Fighters were doing an excellent job on the case, but it was getting complicated, and they needed a little direction. It was time to get organized.

"Okay, Akari and Deshawn, can you two talk to everyone and find out who the witness is, the one who saw the thief with the lunch bag? That way, we have one boy and one girl, just in case," Marybeth said.

They both nodded. Marybeth made a note in her notebook. Turning to Santiago, she waited to see what he would come up with. She didn't want to seem like she was in charge.

"I'll talk to D'Maryea and see if he found out from his mom what she packed in his bag," Santiago said.

After marking that in her notebook, Marybeth looked knowingly up at Ariel.

"Did you follow through with the plan?" Marybeth asked Ariel.

"Yep!" Ariel held up a large plastic bag full of cookies she made last night. "I am going to offer everyone a peanut butter cookie at recess and find out who doesn't take one."

Marybeth made a note of that too.

"Okay, great! It looks like we are ready. I am going to look at the crime scene with my magnifying glass again before everyone puts their lunches away today," Marybeth said.

The Crime Fighters scattered. They all had a job to do to find clues and catch the thief before he, *or she,* could strike again.

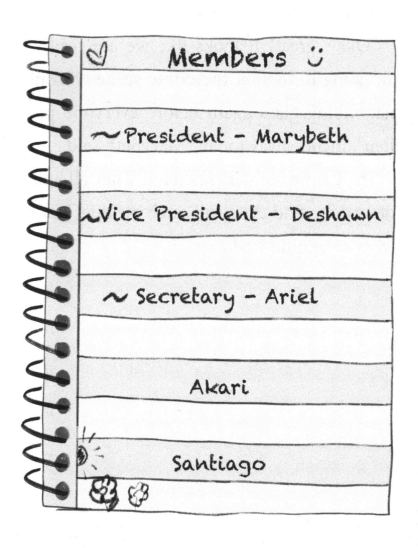

♡ **Members** ☺

~ President - Marybeth

~ Vice President - Deshawn

~ Secretary - Ariel

Akari

Santiago

9
Crime Fighters Club Meeting

During recess the Crime Fighters Club had its first official meeting. They voted Marybeth as president because she had read the most Nancy Drew books. Deshawn was voted in as vice president because he had seen the most crime shows on television. Ariel was unanimously voted in as secretary, since she had the best handwriting. So now she took the notes in Marybeth's notebook.

Everyone started talking at once. Marybeth and Santiago both jumped up at the same time and tried to calm everyone down. Finally, Deshawn let out an impressive whistle. Everyone quieted down at once.

"Quiet! Guys, talk one at a time," Deshawn told them.

The Crime Fighters stopped talking over one another and apologized.

"I think Deshawn should keep order in the meetings. That should be his job as vice president," Marybeth said.

Everyone agreed with Marybeth. Deshawn would keep order during the meetings, partly because he had the loudest whistle.

"Akari, I heard you say something interesting before everyone started talking at once," Deshawn told her.

"Thanks, Deshawn. I was wondering why D'Maryea didn't take a cookie. After all, he had a peanut butter sandwich in his lunch bag," Akari said.

No one had an answer for that. Deshawn turned to Santiago.

"Did you find out what D'Maryea's mom packed in his lunch?" Deshawn asked.

"Yep," Santiago said. "I have a list here. His mom gave him a list of what she could remember. He has almost the same thing today, and he let me see. Except today he has a tuna sandwich."

Santiago passed the list around, and Ariel copied it into the notebook.

The Crime Fighters reviewed the list. Marybeth looked at the clues in her notebook. There was something strange about the class thief, for sure. But what it was—she wasn't sure.

D'Maryea's Missing
Lunch

(NOT MISSING)
1-peanut butter sandwich

1-orange O

1-bag of potato chips

1-sandwich bag of sunflower seeds

1-bag of fruit snacks

1-juice box

1-note from mom
(NOT MISSING)

Marybeth reviewed the list of classmates who had taken cookies. There was a pattern.

"Almost everyone chose a cookie," Ariel reported to the group, checking her notes in the official club notebook. "Noah, Sofia, Santiago, and D'Maryea are the only ones that did not take a cookie. Oh, and Mrs. Stardowski didn't want one either."

"I hope this is all we need to solve the case," Marybeth said. "But I'm afraid it might not be."

THE MYSTERY OF THE MISSING LUNCH

10
The Culprit Strikes Again

"This list has to be the most important clue," Marybeth said.

"Sure," Deshawn said, "but why?"

"We found nothing when we investigated the lunch bag. We did not find anything out from interviewing D'Maryea. We did not learn much from passing out peanut butter cookies. The answer must be in this list," Marybeth said.

"Maybe we should go back and read some

more *Nancy Drew* books," Akari said.

"It couldn't hurt!" Ariel said.

"Look, we have the answer. We just have to put our heads together. Sometimes it just takes time before you solve a case," Marybeth assured everyone.

"Yes, and in the meantime, what if someone else's lunch is stolen?" Santiago asked.

Marybeth did not answer him. She had not thought of that. While she was thinking about it, the bell rang to signal it was time to go inside for reading.

The Crime Fighters Club trudged inside, passing the lunch bags as they headed to their desks. As Marybeth passed the lunch bags, she thought they looked sad. Could lunch bags look sad?

Class passed slowly for Marybeth that morning. She was pretty sure the rest of her friends felt the same way by the looks on their faces. When Mrs. Stardowski called on her during the reading lesson, she gave an answer from her history homework. This did not please either of them.

Finally, it was time for lunch. Marybeth and the other Crime Fighters were tense with worry. Even Mrs. Stardowski seemed less chipper than usual. Following the classroom routine, she released one pod at a time for lunch.

There were eight pods in the class. As each pod was released, Marybeth relaxed. When half of the class was gone, Marybeth thought everything was going to be okay.

"I'm gonna pound someone!"

The students still in the classroom heard the unmistakable yell of the class bully, Mikey Rogers. Mrs. Stardowski rushed to the alcove, but Marybeth had a sinking feeling she already knew what had happened. She exchanged glances with Deshawn, the only Crime Fighter left in the room.

Voices came from the alcove. Mrs. Stardowski tried to calm Mikey down. He was used to being the bully, not the victim. Marybeth shook her head. She did not like Mikey much, but she still felt sorry for him. They would treat him like any other victim.

"Santiago was right," Deshawn whispered.

"I wish he wasn't," Marybeth whispered back.

"Right about what?" Natasha asked. She was the only other person in their pod remaining. Noah, their other pod mate, had been released to the restroom right before lunch.

"Santiago was afraid that there were going to be more lunch thefts before we caught the thief," Marybeth said.

Natasha nodded. Just then, Mrs. Stardowski

released the rest of the class. Marybeth noticed that Deshawn had made a list.

"What is that?" Marybeth asked.

"I made a list of who was in the room when Mikey noticed his lunch was gone," Deshawn said.

Marybeth wished she had thought of that. After all, half of the class was now on the list of suspects—that included half of the Crime Fighters Club too.

11
The Suspects

"It has to be a boy," Akari said.

"It was definitely a boy," agrees Ariel.

"Why? Just because both victims were boys?" Santiago said. "You think it was us? That's not fair."

"I didn't say that," Akari said.

"It could be anyone who wasn't in the room," Ariel said.

Marybeth agreed with Santiago. She looked

at the members of the Crime Fighters Club. They couldn't fight among themselves! Something had to be done and soon.

"I don't think we should decide based on girls and boys. I agree with Santiago," Marybeth said. "Should we vote?"

Everyone thought about this for a few moments. Then they all shook their heads. They decided not to make it a girls-versus-boys problem.

"We need to make a list of our suspects. Ariel, you have the official Crime Fighters Club notebook. Deshawn made a list of the . . . non-suspects. You should record them," Marybeth said.

"Non-suspects?" Akari asked.

"Those are the kids who were still in the room when Mikey noticed his lunch bag was missing," Deshawn explained.

"Oh."

The Suspects

"How do we know none of them is the thief?" Santiago asked.

"Because they couldn't have taken Mikey's lunch. What are the odds that we have two thieves?" Marybeth said.

No one wanted to think that there were two thieves at Edison Elementary School. They all agreed that the person who took D'Maryea's lunch must be the person who took Mikey's lunch. It was simpler that way.

"Isn't it easier just to make a list of the suspects?" Ariel asked.

"Those are the kids in the pods who went to recess before Mikey found his lunch bag missing," Akari said.

"How many are there?" Santiago asked.

"Thirteen," Marybeth said miserably.

"You have to include us too," Akari said.

"Sixteen!" The other Crime Fighters said at once, except for Ariel.

"That's a lot of suspects," Santiago said.

"Actually, it's seventeen," Deshawn corrected.

"Seventeen?" Akari asked.

"Noah was in the bathroom. He wasn't in class when Mikey discovered his lunch missing either."

Seventeen suspects. Would the Crime Fighters ever solve this case? It seemed impossible.

"Could Noah have taken the lunch bag? After all, he was in the bathroom," Santiago said.

"Someone should interview Noah," Marybeth said.

"I will," Santiago said. "Noah is a really nice kid. I am sure he didn't do it. But we should interview him just to cross him off the list."

The Crime Fighters all nodded. Everyone was sure that the quiet and polite Noah would not have taken the lunch bag. After all, how could he when he was in the bathroom?

"Okay, I wrote down the other sixteen names. There are eight boys and nine girls. Here is the list," Marybeth said.

Suspect List

1. Victor
2. Anika
3. Massimilliano
4. Lanxton
5. Jetilat
6. Jasmin
7. Jess
8. Charity
9. Jaedyn
10. Angel
11. Josiah
12. Precious
13. Jorge
14. Akari
15. Santiago
16. Ariel
17. Noah

"Boy, Marybeth," Akari said, "the Crime Fighters Club better not let too many people see that notebook. We will have a lot of people mad at us for making them a suspect!"

There was a round of nodding heads. Marybeth had to agree. She had some friends on that list—not to mention *three* of the Crime Fighters. She wasn't trying to make enemies, either.

"I know! I can't help it. I am just following the facts. The evidence speaks for itself. We can't help who was in the room, can we?" exclaimed Marybeth.

"No, we can't. We are going to have to solve this case fast, though. We can't have all these people under suspicion!" Deshawn said.

Everyone agreed. For the sake of the Crime Fighters and their classmates, they had to find the thief. Innocent lives were at stake.

12
Planning the Trap

The Crime Fighters Club met under a tree in the shade. No one said anything. They chewed in silence. Ariel was especially quiet. She did not think her name should be on the suspect list. How could the secretary of the club be an actual suspect?

"All of us are suspects," Marybeth said.

"I don't know why you keep saying that," Ariel said, glaring at Marybeth. "How can you be our friends and think we would steal?"

"It's not about that," Marybeth said. "It is about facts, not feelings."

"It is a fact that I am not a thief," Ariel said.

"I am not calling anyone a thief," Marybeth said. "We just need evidence."

"I have money for lunch," Santiago said. "My mom gives me money every day."

"Okay, good," Marybeth said, writing it in her notebook. "Did anyone see it?"

Santiago nodded. "Deshawn saw it because I gave him some of it."

"You know I always have a lunch with too much food from the restaurant," Akari said.

Writing all of this down, Marybeth looked around at the others to see if anyone had anything to add. Everyone had a witness to their lunch except for Ariel. She glared at Marybeth.

"This is dumb! Why should I have to prove

anything to you?" Ariel said.

Everyone looked from Ariel to Marybeth. Eventually, they went back to eating. Marybeth wrote in her notebook that Ariel liked sweets. She liked her friend, but everyone was a suspect.

"Whoever this is, the person is mean," Santiago said quietly. "Who crumples up a note from someone's mama?"

This observation had everyone nodding. The thief must be a mean person. None of the Crime Fighters were that mean. It must not be one of them.

"I think we need to set a trap," Marybeth announced.

The Crime Fighters looked at her. The expressions on their faces went from excitement to surprise. Santiago was the one who reacted first.

"Do you know who the thief is?" Santiago

asked.

"No," Marybeth said, "I think we can set a trap, though. We just have to make a lunch bag that no one can resist."

"How?" Akari asked.

"Both victims have been boys," Deshawn said.

"That's true," Ariel said with a nod.

"I noted that," Marybeth said. "I thought we could talk about something really good in either Deshawn's or Santiago's lunch bag. Something that he would love to steal. Something too good to pass up!"

"What good would that do?" Santiago asked. "We haven't caught the thief before. How would knowing which bag the theif would take help us catch the culprit?"

"That's the part I have not figured out yet," Marybeth admitted.

The Crime Fighters brainstormed ways to

set a trap for the thief. Before long, everyone was talking at once, and Marybeth couldn't get it all down in the notebook. She could not even keep track of who said what. So she stopped even trying.

"We can put a mousetrap in the lunch bag. The thief will scream!"

"We can put jelly at the bottom of the lunch bag."

"That's so gross."

"I know. Let's put rotten eggs in there."

"Ewww!"

"Powdered donuts!"

"How about a live snake?"

"No, crickets!"

"Did you say a live snake?"

"Wait! Wait a minute, everyone!" Marybeth looked at Deshawn who knew that meant that he should whistle for order.

Deshawn whistled, and everyone stopped talking. Marybeth sighed with relief. Those suggestions got a little crazy.

"Who said powdered donuts?" Marybeth said.

"I did," Ariel said.

"What's your idea?" Marybeth asked.

"Any time I eat powdered donuts, the sugar gets all over my hands," Ariel said.

The other Crime Fighters nodded. They usually had the same problem with powdered sugar donuts. What a mess!

"My mom always gets mad at me!" Deshawn said.

"Yeah, my mom says I get the mess all over the furniture and my clothes!" Santiago said.

"So, my idea was that we take the donuts out of the package and put them at the bottom of the lunch bag," Ariel said. "Deshawn can leave his lunch bag where the thief can find it. When the thief goes to steal it, we will know!"

The Crime Fighters were excited. Ariel's plan seemed like the perfect trap. The thief was theirs!

"One thing I know—you can't get that sugar off your hands easily!" Marybeth said.

"No, you can't," Deshawn agreed.

"The thief will be whoever has white powdered sugar all over his hands and clothes!" Ariel said.

"His or hers!" Santiago corrected.

Everyone spoke at once. The plan was born. All they had to do was put it into action.

THE MYSTERY OF THE MISSING LUNCH

13
Setting the Trap

The next day, Marybeth and Deshawn came to school early to set up their trap. Deshawn looked up at Marybeth in surprise when he saw her poring over five pages of notes. She had been very busy the night before going over the detailed arrangements again and again.

"Everything has to be perfect!" Marybeth said. "The plan has to go off without a hitch."

"Yes, Marybeth," Deshawn said. "We planned this for a long time yesterday."

"You're right," Marybeth agreed.

Marybeth took a deep breath and tried to calm down. Everyone had a job to do. She and Deshawn had arrived early because theirs was first.

The Crime Fighters' Jobs

Marybeth and Deshawn: *Crumple up powdered donuts in the bottom of Deshawn's lunch bag.*

Akari: *Start a fight with Mikey on the playground.*

Santiago: *Shout about the fight on the playground until there is a crowd gathered.*

Ariel: *Steal Mrs. Stardowski's keys!*

The last job on the list was the scariest of all. After all, if Ariel was caught, she could be in big trouble. Ariel had volunteered for the job to prove her innocence to the club. She knew it was risky, but very important.

It was almost time for school to start. Kids milled around the classroom. Marybeth looked up from her notebook and saw Akari give the signal and head off to the playground. It was showtime!

Deshawn headed into the classroom, put his lunch bag away, and went back out again. Marybeth was the lookout. She stayed in the doorway, making sure that she noticed any kids that walked by and kept her eye on Mrs. Stardowski.

As quick as a flash, Ariel was out the door. She quickly locked it and then gave Marybeth a wink. She held up Mrs. Stardowski's keys and then ran off for the teacher's lounge, where she would leave them on a table.

Marybeth could hear sounds coming from

the playground now. That was undoubtedly where Mrs. Stardowski was. There were no more kids in the hallway now. They had run to the fight.

Since it was safe to go out to the playground, Marybeth followed the rest of the kids. She saw Akari up in a tree with Mikey down below her, jumping up and down, trying to get at her. Akari yelled something at him.

With a grin, Marybeth leaned against the school wall. Things could not be going better. All the kids were distracted.

"He's really mad!"

Marybeth turned around to see Ariel next to her, smiling. She had finished hiding the keys.

"Yep," Marybeth agreed with a smile. Payback could be a lot of fun.

14
Baiting the Trap

Mrs. Stardowski could not find her keys. Marybeth felt sorry for her. The Crime Fighters needed to keep everyone in one place, but they had not meant to do something mean to their teacher.

All of the kids stood in a line in the hallway outside of the classroom, waiting for their teacher. Deshawn and Santiago loudly discussed how good Deshawn lunch was. It was all part of the plan.

"I have such a good lunch!" Deshawn said. "Today is my little brother's birthday."

"What did your mom pack?" Santiago asked.

"Donuts! The best sugar donuts you will ever eat. Would you like one?" Deshawn offered, still talking louder than necessary.

"Oh man, thanks!" Santiago said.

"I also have this great juice box. Grape! She packed me a good sandwich too. I don't remember what kind. Of course, *the donuts* are the important part," Deshawn said.

"Do you have enough to share?" Santiago asked as those kids around him listened closely to the answer.

"Definitely. It may be my brother's birthday, but this is the best lunch I've had *all year*!" Deshawn said excitedly.

Deshawn enjoyed his part of the script. All

the kids around him paid attention. Marybeth tried to observe which kids were most closely watching him without making it look like she was watching them.

The boys had made sure they were in the middle of the line so that kids all around them would hear their conversation. Marybeth, Akari, and Ariel spread out throughout the line. Between them, the three girls were positioned to observe their whole class.

"I found them! Sorry, everybody! Apparently, I left them in the teacher's lounge," Mrs. Stardowski said, as she came hurrying down the hallway with her keys in her hand and opened the door.

The class filed in. Deshawn patted his lunch bag as he walked by. It had his name written on it in bright blue magic marker. Not all of the kids wrote their names on their lunch bags, but

Deshawn wanted to make sure that the thief had no problem finding his.

After she sat down, Marybeth began her morning work, but she found it particularly hard to concentrate. Her eyes kept going over to the alcove and wandering around the room to her classmates to see if anyone else was looking there too. She noticed that Noah seemed distracted.

"Hey, Noah, what's wrong?" Marybeth whispered.

"It's nothing, Marybeth," the shy boy answered. "I just didn't eat much for breakfast this morning."

Marybeth nodded. She hadn't eaten much either. She had been so nervous about putting the plan into action that when her mom put a bowl of oatmeal in front of her, it had not looked at all appetizing. Of course, oatmeal never did.

Smiling, Marybeth reached into her backpack and pulled out a small bag of almonds. Looking over her shoulder to see Mrs. Stardowski busy at her desk, she carefully opened the bag and poured half of them on Noah's desk and the other half onto hers. Then she popped one into her mouth.

"We can't get much work done on a hungry stomach, now can we?" Marybeth said with a smile.

Noah smiled back at her and ate his almonds. Within a few minutes, they had both eaten their share. Marybeth felt better, and she also thought she might have made a new friend.

THE MYSTERY OF THE MISSING LUNCH

15
Springing the Trap

At lunchtime, Mrs. Stardowski let her students out quickly. She released one pod after the other, as if she wanted all her students to get their lunches at the same time. Students crowded the door, so Marybeth couldn't see what happened to Deshawn's lunch bag.

"Did you see who took it?" Marybeth asked Deshawn while trying to peer around the students in the doorway.

Both students held back, waiting until the other students had left before they went up to the lunch shelves. Deshawn shook his head.

The rest of the Crime Fighters were already outside. The plan was for them to take up spots around the playground. Somehow, they were hoping to see who had the lunch bag.

"Look, Deshawn!" Marybeth said, pointing.

Deshawn walked up to the shelf. He saw his lunch bag, but someone had opened it. Both Crime Fighters carefully opened the bag. Inside, everything was still there except the donuts!

"Someone *has* been in here," Deshawn said, pumping his fist into the air.

Marybeth looked. There was powdered sugar all over the inside of the lunch bag and its contents. More powdered sugar speckled the outside of the bag and the shelf.

"We have the thief now!" Marybeth said.

"What was that, Marybeth?" Mrs. Stardowski asked, coming up behind them.

Marybeth and Deshawn turned around to face their teacher, then looked at each other. Deshawn closed his lunch bag quickly.

"Nothing, Mrs. Stardowski," Marybeth said. "Deshawn and I are just so glad that there was no lunch thief today."

"Yes, so am I," Mrs. Stardowski said with relief in her voice. "Marybeth, you and Deshawn should go outside to lunch now."

"Yes, Mrs. Stardowski," Marybeth said.

The two quickly went outside to find the other Crime Fighters. While they were walking, Marybeth pulled a magnifying glass from her pocket.

"Do you really think you'll need that?" Deshawn asked her.

"A Crime Fighter should use the right tools when looking for clues!" Marybeth said.

"Okay," Deshawn said, "where do we start?"

They went out to the playground. Akari, Ariel, and Santiago came up to them. It was clear from their faces that they had not had any luck.

"Nothing?" Marybeth asked.

"I didn't see anything obvious," Akari reported, shaking her head.

"Me either," Santiago said. "No one went to the bathroom to wash the sugar off."

"What do you think, Ariel?" Deshawn asked.

"I hate to say it, but I did see someone acting suspiciously. He had what looked like powdered sugar on his pants," Ariel said, a little reluctantly.

"Who?" Marybeth asked excitedly.

"Have you guys ever noticed that at lunchtime, not everyone eats lunch?" Ariel asked.

16
An Unlikely Thief

"What do you mean, Ariel?" Marybeth asked. "Who doesn't eat lunch?"

Ariel pointed to a tree at the far corner of the playground. They could all see a lone figure sitting under it. From this far away, it was not possible to tell who it was.

"Do you mean to say someone isn't eating lunch today?" Santiago said. "Why?"

"Maybe it's a guilty conscience," Deshawn

said with a bit of aggression in his voice. "We should go find out."

The Crime Fighters walked over to the tree. As they got closer, they could see who was sitting there. It was their classmate Noah.

"Noah, why are you sitting here all by yourself?" Marybeth asked.

Noah looked up. He did not answer her question. Instead, he looked down at his hands.

"I just felt like being by myself," Noah said.

Marybeth sat down next to Noah. Santiago sat on the other side of him. Marybeth thought Santiago was doing his best to look as friendly as possible. The other Crime Fighters sat around them in a circle.

"Noah, can we see your hands, please?" Marybeth asked.

Noah held out his hands. Marybeth did not need her magnifying glass. Powdered sugar covered them.

"Why did you do it, Noah?" Ariel asked in a soft voice. "Why were you taking food from your classmates' lunch bags?"

Noah did not answer her. He just looked down at the grass. Marybeth saw a small tear escape from the corner of his eye.

Santiago put his arm around Noah's shoulder. "It's okay, man. Just tell us why you did it. We know you're not a bad person."

The rest of the Crime Fighters nodded. They knew Noah was no bully. They would never have expected him to be the thief.

"I was hungry," Noah said in a quiet voice.

"You didn't have a lunch?" Akari asked.

Noah shook his head.

"Ever?" Ariel asked in disbelief.

Noah shook his head again.

The Crime Fighters exchanged shocked

looks. How could Noah never have a lunch? Why didn't his mom pack one? Or why didn't he buy one from the cafeteria? Why had they never noticed this?

Marybeth opened her lunch bag and took out half of her sandwich to hand to Noah. Akari gave him a bag of apples. Deshawn gave him a juice box.

"Thanks," Noah said with a smile.

After a few minutes of everyone—including Noah—enjoying their lunch, Noah spoke. "It is pretty cool that D'Maryea's mom writes him notes."

"Yeah, that's really sweet," said Akari.

"If you liked the note from D'Maryea's mom, why did you crumple it up?" Ariel asked.

Marybeth wondered about the crumpled note too. Noah always seemed so sweet. Why would he crumple up a personal note for D'Maryea?

"I dunno. It made me mad that D'Maryea's mom took time to write him something, so I crumpled it. My mom is too stressed out to do that for me," Noah said.

Marybeth wanted to wrap Noah in a hug, but she settled for an awkward pat on the back.

"Does your mom know you would like notes from her?" Ariel asked.

"I've never talked to her about it," Noah said as he twisted some grass around his finger.

"If you tell her how cool you think it is that D'Maryea gets notes in his lunch bag, maybe she'll leave notes in yours," Marybeth said.

Noah couldn't get too upset with his mom. She didn't even know he wanted notes in his lunch. Then again, he didn't even get lunch.

Noah shrugged. "Yeah, maybe."

The Crime Fighters ate in silence, only exchanging a few smiles. After they finished,

Marybeth took out her notebook and wrote case closed. The problem was—it really wasn't.

"Thanks," Noah said with a smile.

The Crime Fighters ate in silence, only exchanging a few smiles. After they finished, Marybeth took out her notebook and wrote *case closed*. The problem was—it really wasn't.

Suspect List

1. ~~Victor~~
2. Anika
3. Massimilliano
4. ~~Lanxton~~
5. ~~Jelilat~~
6. ~~Jasmin~~
7. ~~Jess~~
8. Charity
9. ~~Jaedyn~~
10. ~~Angel~~
11. Josiah
12. Precious
13. ~~Jorge~~
14. ~~Akari~~
15. ~~Santiago~~
16. ~~Ariel~~
17. (Noah) :(

CASE CLOSED

17
Noah's Problem

After school that day, Marybeth did not go home the way she usually did. Her usual routine was to walk with Ariel until the corner, and then take Peach Street for two more blocks to Apricot Blossom Court. Today, she followed Noah.

Noah did not get a lunch bag from the shelf. He did not even get a backpack or book bag from the hooks by the door. He just took his homework folder and walked away from the school down Main Street.

Marybeth was starting to get worried. Her parents did not like her to walk in this direction. The streets were bigger and had too many lanes. There weren't neighborhoods here, only stores.

Getting out her notebook, Marybeth took notes of the route Noah was taking and continued to follow him. He walked down Main Street for five blocks, all the way to City Park. Then he stopped at the parking lot in front of a beat-up white sedan.

Relieved to stop traveling so far from home, Marybeth hid behind a tree. There was a lady in the car. Maybe it was Noah's mom. She must pick him up here and drive him home. Marybeth wondered why Noah's mom hadn't come to the school to get him like the other parents.

Since she was tired from walking for so long, Marybeth scooted down and leaned against the tree. She decided to wait until they left and then go home. The problem was, they didn't leave. Noah and his mom stayed in the car.

Marybeth stayed there so long that she got bored. She finally pulled out her homework folder and started doing some math. It seemed like a good idea to do something productive while she was waiting.

"Marybeth?"

Startled, Marybeth looked up. Noah stood above her, and he looked confused.

"Marybeth, what are you doing here?" Noah asked.

"I'm doing my math homework. How do you reduce thirty-two by four?" Marybeth quickly said.

"Eight," Noah said, "but that doesn't

answer my question."

"Oh," Marybeth said. She stood up, a little embarrassed and unsure how to answer. "I— followed you."

"I kind of guessed that," Noah said. He looked embarrassed too. "Why?"

"I was curious. The Crime Fighters Club wanted to solve the Case of the Missing Lunches. We thought it would be a bully stealing from our classmates. We never thought it would be a nice kid like you," Marybeth said.

"Oh," Noah said, looking at his feet.

"Look, Noah, what is going on? Why are you here, at this park, in a car?" Marybeth had lots of questions. "Why don't you have lunch? Is that your mom?"

Noah nodded.

"Can I meet her?" Marybeth said.

"Why do you want to meet my mom?"

Noah asked.

"Because she's waving at me," Marybeth said with a half-grin while doing a little wave back.

"Oh," Noah said, "okay."

As they walked toward the car, Noah looked at Marybeth. "I never have lunch because my mom and I live in that car. My mom lost her job. It's really hard for us right now."

Marybeth did not know what to say. When she had first set out to solve the missing lunch bag case, she had never expected any of this. Now she was not sure what to do.

"Mom, this is my classmate, Marybeth," said Noah.

"Hello, Marybeth," Noah's mom said.

Noah's mom was very nice. She helped Marybeth with her homework. Noah helped too. He was very good at math.

"Marybeth, does your mom know where

you are?" Noah's mom asked.

Marybeth had forgotten all about the time. Her mom did not know where she was, and she was probably worried. She hoped she could come up with a good explanation for all of this when she got home so she wouldn't be in trouble.

"It is pretty expensive to put gas in the car, so we try not to drive it unless we have to. We don't want your mom to worry about you though, so I think we should take you home now," Noah's mom said.

"Thank you very much," Marybeth said.

18
Resources for the Homeless

The next day, Mrs. Stardowski said that the principal of the school was going to come in and make a special presentation to the class. Marybeth was worried. It had been a busy and unusual week, and special presentations did not happen every day.

"Good morning, class. My name is Dr. Martin. I am sure that most of you know I am your principal. I hope you are all having a good day!" Dr. Martin said.

"Good morning, Dr. Martin," the class recited.

"Class, I am going around to all the classes this month to make this special presentation on Community Resources. Do you know what that means, class? It is a very important topic."

Most of the students in the class shook their heads. Many of them looked puzzled. Marybeth was excited and a little hopeful.

"As a school, it is our job to take care of each other. As a community, we want to take care of the students in the school and their families. This means that we look out for each other. In your classroom, do you take care of each other? Do you look out for one another when someone is hurt or needs help? Is your classroom a community?"

The class had talked about this, and they all nodded their heads. Mrs. Stardowski had reminded them to take care of one another, and they tried to do it. Marybeth felt that the Crime Fighters had done a good job that very week!

"I'm pleased to see so many nodding heads. Sometimes, people need extra help. That is not a bad thing. Everyone needs help sometimes. If you need help, I want you to make sure that you ask for it. You can ask your teacher, or the school secretary, or me, your principal. Never be afraid to ask for help when you need it.

More heads were nodding in understanding.

"I am going to send home some flyers for you to give your parents. Some of these are flyers on community resources such as job-hunting assistance, housing assistance, food banks, and shelters. There is also a flyer on the school lunch program. How many of you know about the school lunch program?" Dr. Martin asked.

A few students raised their hands, but most of them did not. Marybeth did not raise her hand. Most of the students in the class brought their lunches, including her.

"The school provides lunch for any student who wants one. You do not need to pay for it. All you have to do is take this form to your parent or guardian and have it filled out and brought back. This lunch is free, and I can assure you it tastes very good. I eat it myself when I forget to bring a lunch!" Dr. Martin laughed.

Many of the students laughed at this. Marybeth looked at Ariel, who forgot her lunch all the time. She also thought it was very funny to think of the principal forgetting his lunch! What a silly idea.

The principal rubbed his hands together. "Any questions?"

"What if you don't like the lunch?"

D'Maryea asked. "I don't eat peanut butter. My mom *always* forgets."

Marybeth and the others nodded. She realized that's why he didn't take a cookie.

"There will be choices for allergies and preferences," Dr. Martin said.

When the principal left, Mrs. Stardowski taught a lesson on homelessness. She explained that some people did not have a house or an apartment to live in. Sometimes they had to live in a car or a shelter.

Marybeth raised her hand. "Should these people use the flyers that Dr. Martin passed out, Mrs. Stardowski?"

"Yes, Marybeth. It is very important that communities work together to provide resources like the ones in the flyers that Dr. Martin gave us. The school lunch program and food banks are very important resources so that homeless students have food."

D'Maryea raised his hand, and Mrs. Stardowski called on him.

"Do you mean that some of the homeless people are kids like us, Mrs. Stardowski?" D'Maryea asked.

"Yes, D'Maryea. Some homeless kids are in this school. It is very important for kids to be in school, even if they are homeless. We hope the schools can help them by providing resources like school lunch."

The students in Mrs. Stardowski's class did not realize that there could be students in their class who were homeless. They did not want to tease these kids or be mean to them. They wanted to help them.

"How else can we help the homeless, Mrs. Stardowski?" Ariel asked.

"That is an excellent question, Ariel. We can

donate to food banks and shelters. We can also pay attention to our friends and neighbors. When someone needs help, we will know," Mrs. Stardowski said.

Marybeth nodded. She would pay more attention to her friends and classmates from now on. Noah had needed help, and she had not even known it. She would not let that happen again.

THE MYSTERY OF THE MISSING LUNCH

19
The Newest Member

One month later, the Crime Fighters Club sat at a table inside the cafeteria. The weather had turned rainy, and they decided to stay inside today. Marybeth was complaining about an upcoming math test when the newest member of the Club sat down next to her with his lunch.

"I can help you study, Marybeth," Noah said.

"Thanks, Noah! You know I hate fractions.

Multiplying them has got to be so much worse than adding or subtracting them!" Marybeth complained.

"Actually, it's easier. I'll show you," Noah said, "After I eat my lunch!"

Noah pulled a peanut butter sandwich out of his lunch sack.

"Hey, Noah," Santiago said, "I thought you didn't like peanut butter."

"Why did you think that?" Noah asked, taking a bite.

Santiago looked embarrassed. The other Crime Fighters exchanged looks and did not answer. They did not want to bring up Noah stealing from lunches earlier.

"Never mind," Santiago said.

Noah picked up his bag of sliced apples. Just underneath the bag, Marybeth saw a folded piece of paper. She smiled to herself. He must have talked to his mother about leaving notes in his lunch bag—or at least given her the idea.

"So, Noah, how do you like your new apartment?" Ariel asked, changing the subject.

"It's great!" Noah said. "I have my own room."

"How neat," Akari said. "I don't even have my own room. Did your mom start her new job too?"

"Yeah, she's really busy. It's good though. She is much happier. She even sings along with the radio at the top of her lungs all the time now."

They all laughed. Some of their moms did the same thing. It was good to see Noah smile too.

"So, Noah, about those fractions," Marybeth said.

The End

THE MYSTERY OF THE MISSING LUNCH

Resources on Homelessness and Child Poverty for Teachers and Parents:

https://www.feedingamerica.org/

https://pedsinreview.aappublications.org/content/39/10/530

https://datacenter.kidscount.org/

The Author

Jordan Winters

Jordan has always loved solving mysteries and writing. Being a writer allows Jordan to do both! Her advice for all young people is to never give up on your dreams. When you see a mystery, follow it!

Lightning Source UK Ltd.
Milton Keynes UK
UKHW041841090223
416678UK00001B/30